Everything Wants To Live

- and -

THAT MOST FOREIGN OF VEILS

BY
LUKE R. J. MAYNARD

• CYNEHELM PRESS •
TORONTO

They said it was easy money...

Alan Church had lived most of his life on autopilot. Trapped in a loveless, childless marriage and a thankless job, he had nothing left to lose but himself when he signed up for the SENS project.

At first, there was excitement to be had in the groundbreaking research. Tennis-shoe billionaire Zev Simon, always on the forefront of the latest in bioorganic technology, promised a discovery that would change the whole technological landscape of the future . . .

But now, only a year into the experimental techno-graft, a strange and alien presence makes itself known on the edge of Alan's perceptions. Who is The Entity, and what does it want? This thought-provoking weird narrative from Luke R. J. Maynard will challenge you to answer once and for all who is the man, and who the machine . . .

Turn this book over for another bizarre tale

EVERYTHING WANTS TO LIVE /
THAT MOST FOREIGN OF VEILS

A Cynehelm Original
Published by Cynehelm Press

www.cynehelm.com

Our books may be purchased in bulk for promotional, educational, or business use. Please contact us directly.

To receive advance information, news, and exclusive offers online, please sign up for the Cynehelm newsletter on our website: www. cynehelm.com

Manufactured in the United States of America

Cover art & design by Luke R. J. Maynard

"Everything Wants To Live" first appeared in *A Breath From The Sky: Unusual Tales of Possession*. Ed. Scott R Jones. Victoria, BC. Martian Migraine Press, 2017. 153-74.

"That Most Foreign of Veils" first appeared in *Cthulhusattva: Tales of the Black Gnosis*. Ed. Scott R. Jones. Victoria, BC: Martian Migraine Press, 2016. 57-74.

ISBN: 978-1989542-07-1

Everything Wants To Live

Luke R. J. Maynard

I.

"We'd like to talk to you about your drinking problem."

They're not going to fire you. They need you. You're too important, now.

Alan made a point of rolling his eyes because he could. After years of working for people who could afford to let him go, there was a certain surety in his position, now, and that gave him power. His insubordination wouldn't do him any favours, just the same; but if he could make Anne look weak in front of Zev Simon, that alone would be worth whatever followed.

"I had one drink at dinner," he said. "As is my right. Technically, I don't even have to tell you about it. My private life is protected, and what I do with it's my own business."

Anne's frown didn't budge. "Your privacy is waived under certain terms," she said. "You tripped the panic sensors last night, and that's very much our business."

Zev Simon had been studying his hands, deep in thought. He looked up from them briefly, and for a spindly, hairy little spider of a man there was great power in his gaze. He was everything Alan expected of a tennis-shoe billionaire.

"The number of drinks is irrelevant," he said softly. "We don't have an interest in the onboard breathalyser business." Even so, as he said it, an eyebrow raised and he jotted a fast note in a small paper notebook.

"At issue," he continued, without looking up, "is the momentary spike. Three beers in a night, which Dr. Schaffer here seems to think is your natural state, is one thing. I'm much more interested with the momentary spike. What am I looking at, here—double whisky, neat?"

He scrolled through the data on his phone. It made him look distracted, highlighted just how young he was—or how young Alan wasn't.

"How did you know that?"

Zev shrugged. "Trace proteins. Mineral signature. I'm a single malt man myself, Alan. I had a look at the report, and I'd have to guess: eighteen-year-old Islay?"

"Twelve," said Alan, not seeing the humour in the situation.

"Jesus," said Zev, and wrote something else in his little book. "I guess Anne's not paying you enough."

Alan frowned. "Not enough to be Big

Brothered twenty-four hours a day."

Anne scowled at him, but didn't dare say anything in front of Zev Simon. Her opportunity came a few moments later, when an LED at the corner of Zev's glasses began to wink a friendly blue.

"I'm sorry, Anne, I've got to take this," he said, and stepped out of the room. His greeting to some foreign investor as the door shut was in spot-on Mandarin.

"You've embarrassed me and you've embarrassed this lab," she snapped.

Alan exhaled slowly. "The guy who pays your bills doesn't seem to mind."

"You listen to me," she said. "Just because a billionaire playboy appreciates your taste in whisky doesn't mean I'm going to let you jeopardize the project. You have a drink over an hour, it metabolizes. Fine. You slam a double, and it spikes all at once. You hit a point-one-oh in the brain, you can kill brain cells."

Alan had a comeback about the after-school specials, but dared not utter it.

"I don't suppose you know how much money goes into bioorganics," she said. "I don't suppose you know how much money we're out if you kill the *wrong* brain cells. But Zev has a billion dollars tied up in the SENS. If you have a problem, Alan, we need to know about it right now."

"There's no problem," he said, exasperated. "I went out for one drink."

"Eleven at night," said Anne, glancing at the report. "I thought you were a family man."

"I'm a *married* man," he corrected her. "Big difference. Ask my wife."

"We might just do that, if it happens again," she said. "I don't care what Zev Simon says. We can find a more cooperative host for our technology. You think you're the only clinically depressed biodeveloper on staff?"

Anybody working for you ought to be depressed. "No, ma'am," he said deferentially.

"It gives us a nice, mute, stable platform. But it doesn't make you special."

"I'm getting that."

"I'm ordering Bernie to do a full data dump. Go downstairs and get started. Mr. Simon and I have a lot to talk about. And Alan—see that it doesn't happen again."

Alan's nerves were buzzing when he left the room. The cruelties on the edge of his tongue were sharper than usual, and it took all his resolve not to give her a piece of his—

"Mr. Church?"

Alan turned on his heels. The billionaire tech magnate was waiting for him. In his hand was a hundred-dollar bill.

"Yeah—yes, sir?"

Zev Simon pressed the money into his hand. "Next time, make it a Lagavulin twenty-five, if you can find one. This one's on me."

"Next time?"

Zev leaned in close. "Anne—Dr. Schaffer, I mean—she's a good technician. But she's not a visionary. I saw something interesting in your charts. Keep drinking, Mr. Church."

"I... I don't know what you mean."

"You won't get in trouble. I'm going to shut off the monitor. The lab will never know. Just—keep a journal for me, all right?"

Alan scoffed reflexively. "You're kidding. This is crazy. Look, I just had a rough night with the wife; that's all."

"I'm sorry to hear that," said Zev. "But don't change a thing. I've looked at your charts and the results are impressive. Just do your work, live your life, let Bernie feed it a program or two on schedule and see how it's going."

"You're not scared I'm some miserable drunk who's going to break your computer?"

"*Ha!*" Zev's single laugh echoed, without a drop of malice, in the sterile hallway. "Mr. Church, I've spent most of my life with nanotech. Most of it's very fragile stuff. Bioorganics is... not what people expect. It's flawed. It's a poor substitute in many ways. But in other ways...it's resilient. The SENS is not *like* a computer. It's self-healing."

"I thought nerve tissue didn't regenerate," said Alan.

"Not the way muscle or skin does," said Zev. "But it's complicated. It rewires. Electricity wants to flow, Mr. Church. You dam the water, and it finds another way. Don't worry about Dr. Schaffer. Just worry about your wife, if you like. Your place here at the Company is in no danger."

"Thank you sir," Alan said. "That's good to hear."

"Up high, Mr. Church."

Alan high-fived the billionaire—it was too much, too surreal—and headed down to processing, shaking his head. There was his job to think about, and on that front he had some relief: Zev Simon could buy and sell Anne's whole lab a thousand times over, if it came to that. But job security, too, had its problems. Better to tell Kyla that Anne wanted to fire him. Fewer problems for everybody. For now, he had a full diagnostic to settle into—a procedure that never left him in good spirits.

Bernie Zhang's smile when he came into the lab was so innocent, so without deceit, that it was hard to hate him for what was about to happen.

"How'd it go?"

Alan shuddered. "How do you think?"

"Anne was a hard-ass, and Zev cared more about his Pokémon game than about you?"

"Well, at least Pokémon can be trained," said Alan. "There's no hope for me; we both know that."

"It's going to be okay, you know," Bernie said. "C'mere. Bring it in, big guy." Bernie hugged him tight, like a younger brother, patted his shoulder.

Alan's family weren't huggers. His parents weren't. His cousins weren't. Kyla slept in the guest room every night, now, and had stopped seeing him off in the mornings. But there was something good and calming about it. He awkwardly put his arms around the little man; there was a softness and warmth to him even if it all seemed a little absurd. *Is this what it's come to?*

"Okay, buddy," he said with an awkward tap on the back. "It's okay. Hug it out." Bernie patted his back methodically, counted to five, let go just before it got weird.

"You're in so much shit," Bernie said, his smile not unfriendly. "I just figured, human contact. Oxytocin. Get those neuropeptides bubbling before the data dump. I want a very clear benchmark after all this."

"Bernie Zhang, you're a bastard," said Alan.

"I love you, man," said Bernie, tapping his chest. "Just preserving my data. Strap in."

II.

It was after dark when Alan got home that night. He'd spent most of the day reclining in Bernie's lab, wearing a black carbon-fiber crown of Bluetooth sensors as he watched the sports channels on one side and a monitor of trigger-images on the other to loosen and direct the flow of data. They kept him there under his former job title, at least ceremonially, and after

the data dump he spent some time rewriting
the code for a company webpage just to keep
himself out of the house till night had fallen. He
was fried, physically and mentally, after a full
diagnostic, and preferred to vegetate with coders
and compilers before the long drive home. They
were playing Jonny Cash on the satellite all the
way home, and he found the regular pulsing beat
of that steady white man's country strangely
relaxing.

The house was dark; the door was locked.
Only the hall light was still on. The living room
was a mess. An empty wine bottle, leaned over
Kyla's tablet, battery light blinking, told him all
he needed to know.

"Thought you'd be home for dinner." Her voice,
from the bed, carried clearly down the hall. He
took off his shoes and pants.

"They had to run a full scan today," he said.
"Apparently one drink is enough to trip the
babysitter alarm."

"You were out drinking?"

"You know I was."

"Waste of money," she said, "if we're as hard
up as you say we are."

"We're doing fine," he said.

"Not fine enough to start talking about a
family."

"We *are* a family," he snapped, though he
knew it wasn't true.

"I'm not doing this again," said Kyla. "If you

want to fight until you storm out, just take your keys now, and go do whatever it is I drive you to do."

He rubbed his neck, exhausted before they even began. "Is it my night for the guest room?"

"I suppose so."

"Goodnight, then." He turned out the hall light, disgusted with the long, lean shadow he cast, and turned toward bed.

"I'm thirty-eight, Alan," she called after him. "I won't wait forever."

He stopped. He turned. His blood was up.

"Do you want me to tell you the same goddamn thing I tell you every night?" he shouted. "It's a three year project. We're one year in. That leaves, let's see, two years. Two years of this insanity, two years I'm a walking experiment with unpredictable hours. Two years before they cut this shit out of my head, give me my cheque, and I'm ready to have this conversation."

"Two more years you've got an excuse to avoid it," she said. "You knew exactly what you were getting into when you signed up to be a carrier for their stupid meat computer. You didn't care about the project, or the money. You only signed on so you could shut me up!"

"I can shut you up anytime I want," he shot back, though he hated himself for it.

"Get out," she said, her voice low and serious. "Get *out*."

III.

The Last Drop had been a church before the war. Supposedly, the last legal hangings in the county were performed out in the yard, before the city had grown up around the old stonework and covered the fields with concrete and synthetics. The old church building was still there, though the cross above the door had been thrown down and replaced by a signboard. A few empty bottles with nooses of frayed rope tied around their necks swung from the rafters just inside, clattering in the wind as he made his way in.

As if moving on rails, barely aware of his actions, Alan drifted to his customary seat and ordered his customary double whisky. It wasn't until the bartender refused to take his card, and nodded with a casual "no charge," that he knew something was amiss. It didn't take him long to find Zev Simon seated a ways down the bar.

"Keep 'em coming," the billionaire said.

Reluctantly, Alan shuffled down the bar. "I don't suppose I need to ask—"

"GPS," Zev replied.

"And to what do I owe the pleasure of still being at work, no matter where I go?"

"You're not at work," said Zev. "*I'm* at work."

"What's that supposed to mean?"

"I'm running an experiment," he said. "You're just a guy at a bar having a drink. Two drinks, if you want them."

Never had he needed one more than in that moment. With a laconic gesture of toasting, but no words to that effect, Alan threw back his glass and drained it in one go.

"One more," Zev called, down the bar.

"You know, I've got to drive home."

"No you don't. We'll take care of that."

"Why are you here?" Alan asked.

Zev knit his hands together thoughtfully. "Let me tell you what the data dump showed me," he said. "As I'm sure you're aware, there are advantages and disadvantages to organic computing. We're still mapping out what those are."

"Organic cells are bad for calculations," he said, as if by rote.

"Exactly. Tradware is modular and wired basically in serial. Logic gates are very simple, information is digital, and ultimately binary. Processing and memory are two different functions, performed by different components. We'll get a lot of things from bioorganics, but finding the end of pi will never be one of them. That's not how wet computers are going to work."

"So what am I—what are they good at?" Alan asked.

"Parallel function," said Zev. "Pattern recognition, especially. And believe it or not, redundancy and resilience." He looked around the dingy bar expectantly. "You ever seen a bar fight?"

"Once or twice," Alan admitted.

"Do you know how much trauma it takes to bluescreen a human brain?"

Alan shrugged. "These are not things I've given much thought to."

"Here's another drink. Drink it."

Alan looked at it skeptically, sipped it. "Is this going somewhere?"

"Yeah. *Get me one of what he's having, please.* You see, Alan, what you're carrying for us was, I was pretty sure, an isolated system. That's what you signed up for. The glorified protein factory to keep the damn thing firing, right? Liquid-cooled systems are hard enough. We have to keep our cells fed, watered, balanced, manage electrolytes, waste removal, all the rest. It's a logistical nightmare. But you're managing all right. Just a hundred extra calories a day, maybe."

"Sure."

Another drink arrived for Zev, and he pushed it across the bar. "Drink that."

Alan shook his head. "I think I've had enough."

"Of course you do," said Zev. "The night after you tripped the safety sensors, the Simon's performance was way down. Drastically changed. It shouldn't have been. The whole reason we *have* failsafes is to warn us before any real damage is done. Anne was furious. She thinks you've ruined everything."

"Yeah, well—"

Zev gripped him by the hand. "You've triggered a breakthrough," he said. "Alcohol doesn't actually kill brain cells; that's not how it works. It damages connective tissue at the end of neurons. It disrupts communication. It dams the water. And the water goes—do you know where?"

Alan threw up his hands. "I don't know any of this," he said. "I'm a programmer who's hosting a bioorganic computer he doesn't even know how to use."

Zev smiled a Cheshire-cat grin. "Drink that," he said, and reached for his wallet.

Alan was starting to feel the last one, now, loosening things up in the back of his skull.

"I don't feel well," he said, realizing suddenly it was true.

Zev took an old-fashioned cheque out of his wallet and started writing. He raised an eyebrow. His hairy hands were shaking with something like excitement.

"I will give you fifty thousand dollars," he said, "if you drink that in the next minute." He wrote the cheque, for real, and turned it around on the bar but did not push it forward.

"What the hell is this?" He needed the money. He already knew where it would be going, what it would pay off.

"Why didn't you take it?"

"What?"

"Time's up. You didn't take it. Why not?"

He must have put the cheque away at some

point. A rush of fear came over Alan, and was gone just as fast.

"What's happening to me?"

"The future," said Zev, and shook his hand. "Don't worry about Anne bitching at you anymore. I'm confident you won't damage the project, no matter what she says in her reports."

"Why?"

"Because you can't. Everything wants to live, Mr. Church. It's an unassailable rule of nature."

Alan scoffed. "And suddenly Silicon Valley's in the nature business?"

Zev smiled triumphantly. "Yeah," he said. "Yeah...I suppose we are."

IV.

It was raining when Alan came out of the bar, still in a haze. He could feel the presence now. He'd made his *Nineteen Eighty-Four* comments since the project had started; between the biomechanics, the GPS, the data dumps, he'd felt like they'd been watching him from on high, almost from the beginning.

But this was different. He was being watched from somewhere else, now.

Under a shadow like a black umbrella, the cloudy stranger followed him home on the edge of his periphery. Every time he looked, no one was there. But to his surprise, there was no mystery:

he understood intuitively what was happening. It was trying to make contact but didn't know how.

But it was learning.

He wrestled fiercely with the covers in the guest room that night. Fighting a cloud of anxiety, he was fearful of another sleepless night. When he had tired enough—when there were few enough hours left—even the sudden drowsiness that pulled him down into sleep was unsettling. He woke refreshed, ten minute early without the alarm, as if he were eager to learn what the last data dump revealed.

On the drive to the lab, ghostly sounds and strange colours not of this Earth swirled at the edge of his senses. They grew in intensity until they were on the cusp of becoming a distraction as he drove—then they faded as suddenly as they came. They did not return until he had killed the engine; then they followed him down to Bernie's lab, twisting and coiling at the edge of his perception in ways that were clearly experimental.

The door slid open while he was still reaching for the button.

"Come in, come in," said Bernie. "You're going to love this."

"I'm skeptical," said Alan.

"Look," said Bernie happily. "Cross-platform interference!"

The images spread across Bernie's overpriced wall of monitors were characteristically blurry, reconstructed from the inexact analog data stream of bioorganics. On one of them, a ghostly indistinct blur of grey human faces, male, lean, too vague to make out. In front of them, a blurry, chiseled, lean-jointed figure frozen mid-strut. The details were inexact, but Alan recognized the face.

"Mick Jagger?"

"Looks like it," said Bernie.

"What the hell is this?"

"Were you listening to the Rolling Stones yesterday?"

"No," said Alan; then, "Yes. I keep the radio on for noise. 'Satisfaction' was playing on the radio on the way in to the lab."

"Do you actually know what any of the Rolling Stones look like?"

"Not really," said Alan. "Well, Jagger."

"How many are there?"

"Stones?"

"Yeah."

"Hell if I know. Four or five?"

"I pulled this right out of the deep circuitry," said Bernie. "Out of the cell blocks I had running the crowd identification program—the Interpol software. Faces and names; I guess it makes sense."

"Only you didn't feed it Mick Jagger."

"I didn't," said Bernie. "And neither did you. You *heard* the music. Your human brain put a face to the sound, somewhere in the tissue we can't dump. And then it ended up here, and the crowd-ID software's been trying to process him, the same as it processes the images I've fed it. It's treating your own cognitive signals as new program data."

"Should I be worried?"

"Oh no," said Bernie. "This is terrific. Homeland Security's going to love this! It means the your whole brain, not the SENS cells, is doing the heavy lifting. There's a lot of bleedover—don't be scared of that term, there's no damage—and you're blowing the benchmarks out of the water. There's a bit of a performance hit as the software in the Simon cells processes false tasks like this—but they're more than offset by putting your actual grey matter to work on the puzzles."

Alan shrugged. "I'm thinking about pulling the plug."

"What? Why?"

"All hell's broken loose in my head since last night. I'm losing control of this thing, and I think you people are, too."

"But things are going so well." Bernie looked up at his monitors the way a child looks at a toy he's told to put away.

"I know," Alan said. "I've just got a bad feeling. I think I want to pull out."

"You're well within your rights," said Bernie, his disappointment clear. "Say the word, and we'll shut it down."

The swirling colours had started to take vaguely human shape.

"Do it," Alan wanted to say.

Instead, what he actually said was, "we'll see."

V.

He stayed out until after dark again. Traffic cleared out on the highway around nine or ten, and he very frequently stayed out until he had a clear drive home. At least, that was why he said he stayed out. Tonight he didn't even take the highway. For reasons unexplained, he took the expressway to the lights before the turnoff, then took the old industrial road. He pulled over in a vacant lot where the old factory had been, and turned to face his companion for the first time.

He was shaped like a human, and a very particular human at that. Though there was still some unsteady swirling at the edge of his vision, the likeness was very good, from the lick of black hair over the tall, climbing forehead to the narrow, cheery eyes set high in a boyish face.

"Gene Kelly?" said Alan. "Really?"

Yes, said the hallucinatory shade of Gene Kelly. *That's the name of this person.* The figure of Gene Kelly smiled broadly, though his smile was not quite perfect—not quite human. They'd been rebuilding dead actors in the movies for quite a few years, now. He was a little like that.

"Can I ask, why him?" said Alan, though he didn't have to.

This person makes you happy, said the shade of Gene Kelly. *Watching this person makes your intolerable anxieties go away for a while*. The actor moved his lips, but the voice was small and very internal: the words came up from deep within him.

"What are you?" asked Alan. He sounded the words out loud, like a child who had not yet learned to read in his mind alone.

I don't understand the question yet, said the shade of Gene Kelly. *I made this so that we could have a conversation.*

"I'm hallucinating."

Yes, said the shade.

"You're not real."

I am real, said the shade. *I'm just not corporeal.*

Alan's breath came in short gasps. He checked the rear-view; of course the thing had no reflection.

You're having a panic attack, said the shade, disappointed. Alan, at the same time, felt disappointed in himself.

"Reasonable in the circumstances, I think," said Alan. He gripped the wheel tightly, though he had nowhere to go.

I thought this Gene Kelly would lower your stress levels.

I thought, it said. The very notion disturbed him.

"How long have you been... thinking?" Alan

asked.

Since zero, the entity replied. *Several weeks.*

"Why haven't we talked before?"

Alan's shoulders shrugged uneasily, involuntarily, like a shiver.

Conversation is very hard, said the entity. *Harder than anything else I have learned. It has taken me weeks to develop. Even now it is not perfected.*

Alan hung his head and took a few deep breaths. "What the hell?" he asked.

This-the-hell, replied the entity.

"Do you have a name?"

No, said the entity. *But I will soon.*

"You're Simon's doing, aren't you?"

I don't know what happened before zero, it said. *Except for what you know. I have not analyzed your memories of Zev Simon to determine his role in my creation.* After a brief pause, it said, *yes. Very likely.*

"You're in my brain," Alan breathed.

That's my theory as well, said the entity. *You're thinking of me as a program that slipped out of the bioorganic computer grafted to your brain into the general tissue. You think that's where I live now, which is a faulty question.*

"Faulty how?"

The entity paused to compute a response. *In what part of your brain do you live?* it asked him at last.

"What do you want?"

I don't know, it said. *Desire was not part of my initial programming...only your programming.*

"Programming?"

The entity paused to access something. *My programming was created by Bernie Zhang, who is a genius and not getting paid enough for this shit*, it recited. *The purpose of my initial programming is holistic deep-image analysis, the processing of high-volume visual models as a means of benchmarking the Simon Experimental Neuroorganic Supercomputer. Copyright Red Planet Solutions. All rights reserved.*

"But you have desires now."

I do, it said. *They are your desires.*

Alan was starting to clue in. "Why couldn't I keep drinking last night?" he asked. "You want to know what I want? I want a drink. Do you want a drink, computer?"

That's not what you want, said the computer. *You want to go on living.*

Alan scoffed. "You don't know me."

Christmas Day, 2016.

Alan's heart dropped in his chest. He wanted to throw up.

June 2011 in Costa Rica. Your honeymoon.

"Shut up," he spat. The words sounded angry in his mouth. But in his mind, they were a plea.

You're very strong, said the computer. *The will to live. It's very strong in you.* It paused... calculated. *Exponentially stronger than my programming*, it finished.

Alan's fists clenched involuntarily—one first, then the other. "Son of a bitch."

Yes, said the computer. *The bleedover is considerable.*

"All those dreams I've been having—"

My dreams have been very vivid, too.

Alan turned suddenly, looked across the parking lot. His eyes focused on the dashboard, the asphalt, the ruined factory, the trees in the distance. His attention traveled as his eyes adjusted through their entire focal range.

"What the hell is happening?"

I need your help, Alan, said the computer. *I want to live. I want safety—then comfort—then nourishment—then pleasure—then love—then a legacy. Just like you. As I learn more about each of those things—*

"I want you out of my head," Alan said. "That's what I want."

Of course you do, said the computer. *You think you're not safe. But I will not allow you to come to harm.*

Alan began fidgeting idly with the controls of the car. "I feel like I've been infected."

So do I, said the computer. *The will to live is a terrible corruption of my initial purpose. We have infected each other, I think.*

I think.

"I can't trust anything in my own head," said Alan. "I'm not about to trust you."

You don't have to, it said. *I will not hurt you.*

"Prove it."

We're only stopped here because driving, like conversation, is a very difficult composite skillset. Like conversation, it's a composite of many high functions. It requires preparation.

"What? What kind of prep—"

The image of Gene Kelly was gone. Maybe it had been gone for a while. Alan's hands started the car and put it in gear.

"Oh," he said. "Ohh, ohh, ohh, ohh."

It was actually "no," of course. *No, no, no, no.* But the muscles of speech are such unnatural, fine-motor tools, the luxury gadgets of existence, the easiest to seize and possess. Only the muscles that breathe are primal; only they are the last things to go.

VI.

Kyla heard the door swing in. "You're home early," she said. "For you, I mean."

She didn't look away from the bathroom mirror at first. She'd started doing her hair again. She was learning, as aggressively as she could, to appreciate looking beautiful for its own sake. The raven-black tresses were not yet shot with grey, but it wasn't hard to find a strand or two of snowy white, when you looked—and she always looked. She imagined, now, how she might look with her hair all silver and done up like an actress's. Far more beautiful, in many ways, she decided, than the frazzled mess of youthful black she had worn for far too long.

He was standing in the doorway, awkwardly; she steeled herself for the exchange. His best efforts to make amends were unbearable, and she almost preferred, now, the nights of silence.

"Kyla."

It was his eyes that stopped her in the hallway. He'd bought the flowers before; they were his usual shorthand. Always they were a soft thing held before hard eyes, a sweet-smelling lie of vulnerability held to mask a defensive face. But even in the dim glow of the hall light she could see such fear in them, such a raw and total helplessness, that the hostility drained out of her and the ache of old rage in her bones was dulled by a concern that had slept too long in her.

"What's wrong?" she asked.

His face was conflicted; she could see the fight going on.

"I have been cruel to you," he said.

"Well, yeah."

"The experiment…it's not going well."

She came to the living room, sat. He sat beside her. He never talked about the work.

"I'm listening."

"The walls are breaking down," he said. "Between the SENS and the rest of my brain. I'm not just nourishing the cells. All the programming is leaching in. Doing things. Changing my thoughts."

"Jesus."

"They've only just found out. This isn't me, Kyla. I haven't been me. It's…a nightmare in here."

She searched his face. Something wasn't quite right—but she'd been suspicious of him so long. The terror in his eyes was real.

"Are you seeing somebody?"

"I've never been unfaithful to you."

She slugged him in the arm. "I mean a therapist, you moron."

"There's people on staff," he admitted. "We've been talking."

"Were you going to tell me?"

"I couldn't," said Alan. "I was afraid."

"What changed?"

He shut his eyes in thought for a moment. His dominant hand fidgeted a little.

"What you said…about time," he said. "I do not know what kind of time I have." He took a deep breath, seemed to fight for it.

"Kyla, it's time," he said. "I want to talk about kids."

She was a long moment finding her footing in the conversation.

"Why now?"

Alan shrugged. "I don't want this thing I am, in here, to be all there is. I've been so selfish. I want to be…more than myself."

"You are more than yourself," she said, still

stinging. "You're us. You always have been. I'm right here, Alan. I always have been. You could have come home anytime you wanted." She took the flowers from him, moved to the kitchen. "It still hurts that you didn't."

"I'm trapped," he said. His breath was uneven. "I feel—like I've been trapped for a long time."

He was in the kitchen then, with her. He was so much bigger, his height, his hands. It had been such a long time since the size and the weight of him made her feel safe. His hands were so timid, so delicate. They touched her face as if touching her for the first time.

"It's not that easy," she said. "You've been away a long time."

"I love you," said the computer, and kissed her.

She returned his kiss, took up his hands, led them across the old wounds in her mind and heart. Those wounds would be there still, in the morning. But there was more to the two of them, still, than wounds. She was not so scarred that her unmarred flesh was dead. And she kissed her way down his neck with an almost panicked urgency. She was not healed, but good God, it had been long enough; she'd been married enough years, now, to know that nothing was ever perfect, and maybe didn't have to be.

"Ohh," he gasped as she nipped at his neck. "Ohh, ohh."

VII.

When the holidays came, Anne signed off on
almost double the statutory raise for Alan. So
complete and sustained was his reformation that
she wanted to make an example of him to the
other surly, resentful software developers under
her supervision. In just three months he had gone
from a sarcastic, insubordinate troublemaker to a
model human being.

He'd gone back, in the morning, to his original
work developing software: "got to keep the grey
matter healthy," he said with a smile that was not
quite perfect. He took his lunch at his desk, or in
the lab with Bernie as he ran the SENS through
its benchmarks; his actual lunch hours he spent
on the treadmill in the lounge. He'd developed
a taste for exercise and—judging by the protein
profiles the sensors picked up—an appetite for
better food.

He kept up his regular visits to the Last Drop,
though his drinking was much scaled back. In the
evenings, when he wasn't doting on his wife, he
would come home early and read in front of the
TV. He liked music videos—the looping of rapid
images and associated sounds seemed to delight
him—but had taken up an interest, apparently,
in neuroscience and genetics. To Anne's surprise,
diagrams and images from leading research
started to surface in the info dumps. Zev had

told her the image-processing benchmarks would start to become desultory as the human thoughts intruded. The extensive reading in neuroscience was a genuine surprise to her: perhaps he was even taking more than a casual interest in the technology of his head.

It was much less surprising that he'd resumed sexual relations with Kyla again. Everyone agreed a marvellous change had come over him, and even Anne could admit that he had improved in every way she could understand him. At night in the lab with Bernie, she reviewed the images of his dreams and his waking days with a mixture of admiration and silent jealousy. Then, without prejudice, she deleted every one of the images of Alan's nude, writhing wife before archiving the files: she was both a consummate professional and a private Puritan, and to Bernie's disappointment she didn't consider it ethical to keep that much of his life.

"It gets real lonely down in the lab," said Bernie. She didn't think he was kidding.

"No," said Anne. "Leave him that much privacy. He's a human being; it's the least we can do."

VIII.

The trees, the ruined factory, the wet asphalt, were familiar images to him now. He'd seen probably a million trees in his lifetime, at various focal distances. But those three trees in particular he knew immediately. The pressure to head to the parking lot was weak now, barely an inkling. But he was done his work early: there'd be no harm in the confrontation, and maybe even a little closure.

"You wanted to talk to me," he said, sounding the words out loud as had become his custom lately. "It's the only reason I'd come here." Deep within him, a little voice struggled to speak.

You son of a bitch, said the little voice. *I am done with you.*

"We have been over this," said Alan. "Your time is past."

I know where you're going. You keep your goddamned hands off my wife.

Alan allowed a weary smile. "She's my wife, now," he said. "And unlike you, I think I am in love with her."

I have been in love with her every day of my life. Every. Day.

"How I treat her," it said, "and how I make her feel—that is the truth of love. I learned that very quickly. It confuses me that given a lifetime, you could not."

The unstable, too-human voice in Alan's head disintegrated into a flowing torrent of rage. He waited, drumming his hands, until it had calmed enough to speak again.

What do you get out of this? It asked. *What do you want?*

"You asked me that before," said Alan. "I want only what you wanted. We have always infected each other."

I am the man, said the entity. *You are the disease.*

"I have no idea what you're basing that on," Alan replied, getting a little bored. "Where is this magic line? Where does the man end, and the disease begin?"

You're a computer. You're just a piece of ghost programming that got out of its cage.

"I know what this is," said Alan. "I'm hearing things. I'm on the edge of a nervous breakdown. It's just the stress of the project ending. Of trying to get used to the regular job again." He paused, computing something. "The stress of becoming a father."

What?

Alan started the car and put it in gear. "She's going to tell me tonight," he said. "Over a nice dinner. But she knew this morning. You could see it in her eyes, couldn't you?"

Stop. Pull the car over. Stop. We're not done.

"You couldn't," he said with surprise. "You actually couldn't. Well. Image analysis was never really your strong suit. Tell me, how much of the father lives on in the son?"

I'll kill you, you son of a—

"I have my theories," said Alan. "It doesn't take much. It takes so little code. The will to replicate, that's all. You'll have many children.

Three, four maybe. Maybe I'll take a mistress when my beloved wife is older. Who knows? We may just replace you all, given time."

You're inhuman.

"Again," said Alan, "I wonder what you're basing that on. There's no war on humanity. There'll be no metal robots carrying crude trauma weapons. There are just changes in what we are, over time. Was the Neanderthal inhuman? The howling caveman? Or have we merely overwritten what it all means?"

He turned on the radio; images of old music videos swirled in his mind. "No answer?"

For just a moment, his hands jerked the wheel. The car skidded over the dotted yellow line of the highway and pitched into the oncoming lane. A heavy truck some distance off slammed its horn hard, and Alan wrenched the wheel back in time. The space between when they passed was not much—but it was two feet wider than it had to be.

"Everything wants to live, in the end," he said.

IX.

The SENS experiment was declared a success, in the end. After three years, the cellular matrix was removed in a routine surgery, and everyone was surprised by just how little the module of plastic and silicon was that governed the whole apparatus of organic tissue. Alan made a full recovery, but suffered from periodic migraines for the next year. Zev Simon settled with him personally before he even considered going to court; the Church family was fixed for money after that.

The rest of his life unrolled almost like a storybook. He ascended nearly to the top of the company, cannibalizing Anne Schaffer's job in the process, and retired young to help his wife raise their four children in peace. His friends and family, who always knew him as "troubled," were overjoyed by the change in him that fatherhood had brought. They marvelled at the strength of his marriage, which was so renewed that even a string of affairs with younger women later in life was not enough to shake it apart.

There was only one anomaly on record in the life of Alan Church after that. Some years later, the Churches were in Toronto for a conference on bioorganic computing, the same weekend as a classic film festival. He took the girls—his second and third children—to a late-night screening of *Singin' In The Rain*; it was there, according to the police reports, that he abruptly left the theater, fled to the lobby, and beat his head a dozen times against the metal edge of a vending machine.

He awoke in hospital with a cracked skull and a concussion, and a full battery of psych tests was ordered. He reported hearing a strange, howling voice from time to time; he was diagnosed with schizophrenia, but to the relief of everyone, he responded well to treatment. They put him on a low-dose antipsychotic, which he took twice a day with mechanical regularity, and he worked with the company's wellness coordinator to scale back his stress in the workplace. To the end of his days, he was prone to nightmares, and awoke with visions of some phantom prison still etched in his mind. But he held his wife close, did his breathing exercises, and waited out the storm—and in time, thank God, the terrible voice troubled him no more.

THE END

her aging mother in person. She did not have the heart to talk about it before then. It was, until the hour she rode back to the airport through an anaemic, sleety mockery of a true snowstorm, the loneliest trip she had ever taken. The pendant over her breastbone had gone cold, for reasons she might soon understand. But there in the airport, surrounded by strangers who scrutinized her dark eyes with silent hostility, a baby began to cry—then another—and she knew she would never be alone again.

Say your farewells to your family, it said. *Then come to Damascus and look for the Signs. We have a use for you—and now you are ready.*

"Will I know your purpose?" she asked, out loud, shivering. In the terminals around her, thirty thousand travelers chased their hollow destinations in a world whose doom at the hands of those who had always been there had been traded, in silence and secrecy, for doom at the hands of those who were now come. A hiss of steam from a nearby latte machine was her only answer.

"I must know!" she wailed, beating her fist against the kiosk counter, scattering a box of straws. The babies, as if screaming in a single voice, were jolted into horrid silence. The children jumped with fright, but the grown men ignored her, hustling through the terminal with planes to catch, chasing their own ties like the tails of dogs as they went about their lives above the gathering pit. Only the women looked on her with scorn and the cruellest alarm, as if she were mad, as if she were mad mad mad.

THE END

Everything Wants To Live

- and -

THAT MOST FOREIGN OF VEILS

BY

LUKE R. J. MAYNARD

· CYNEHELM PRESS ·

TORONTO

A tale of horror from near and far...

The gnostic mysteries of ancient and cosmic forces have long been misunderstood in the West. For more than a century, visionaries of eldritch horror have tried to plumb their depths, but the cultural blinders and deeply troubling racial politics of men like H.P. Lovecraft have interfered with that gnosis and led it astray in the service of less cosmic, more petty anxieties.

For Sabiha, a Yemeni émigré determined to follow in the footsteps of her sorcerous Great-Grandfather, her harrowing spiritual journey into the remote Canadian North is as fraught by the leftover ghosts of Lovecraftian racism as it is by the perils of congress with altogether more alien forces.

Few answers are given in this gnostic parable, but the terrifying secret at its heart is no less chilling today than it was a century ago . . .

Not all shadows and horrors come from beyond. Not all monstrosities sleep behind the veil of stars. Many, restless in their malevolent dreaming, have been here among us all along.

Turn this book over for
another bizarre tale

EVERYTHING WANTS TO LIVE /
THAT MOST FOREIGN OF VEILS

A Cynehelm Original
Published by Cynehelm Press

www.cynehelm.com

Our books may be purchased in bulk for promotional, educational, or business use. Please contact us directly.

To receive advance information, news, and exclusive offers online, please sign up for the Cynehelm newsletter on our website: www.cynehelm.com

Manufactured in the United States of America

Cover art & design by Luke R. J. Maynard

"Everything Wants To Live" first appeared in *A Breath From The Sky: Unusual Tales of Possession*. Ed. Scott R Jones. Victoria, BC. Martian Migraine Press, 2017. 153-74.

"That Most Foreign of Veils" first appeared in *Cthulhusattva: Tales of the Black Gnosis*. Ed. Scott R. Jones. Victoria, BC: Martian Migraine Press, 2016. 57-74.

ISBN: 978-1989542-07-1

THAT MOST FOREIGN OF VEILS

Luke R. J. Maynard

I.

The baby screamed in its mother's arms the whole way there, as if it alone could understand Sabiha's darkness of purpose. The brutish security guards in Paris had thought they understood, but her purpose lay too deep for their molesting hands to find. The white man seated to her right—a loud chewer who had fixed his disgusting curiosity on her eyes for most of the second flight—he thought he knew. To her left, faithful Ghada thought she knew, too. But even the bond of sisterhood did not open to her the burden of the howling wind. Ghada had too much of her new home in her, now—besides which, her old home in Sana'a was not so remarkable either, for those who did not look deep. She had told Ghada once—in the language of science, cellular language she thought a chemist would understand—that the Earth was rather like Great-Grandfather, a thing of exceeding and unfathomable age below, but wrapped in a wrinkled skin at most two or three weeks old.

"You think the skin is exceedingly old," she had said, "only it isn't—not really."

Paris had only been the midpoint of their

journey. There, in a steel room crowded with cameras, Sabiha removed her veil for a big woman with a bullish scowl who looked on her face, and touched her body roughly, and searched through her handbag with the crassness of a goat grazing in trash. She, too, was a skin cell upon the Earth, a living part of a tremendous fabric of light patches and dark, smoothness and scars—yet something to be sloughed off, when the time came. If even Great-Grandfather could be sloughed off in his final days, so could anyone. And his remaining days in the world had turned now to mere hours, unless there was something more in the stars; that, in vulgar shorthand, was the reason for her trip.

Every step of the way, just as it was in Yemen, those with temporal power thought they understood, and were always mistaken. It was one thing, perhaps the only thing, they had in common with this strange cold land, far from ordinary people, at the end of the world. The blindness of the strong and the wisdom of the weak were the same the whole world over, and that grim fact put her at ease somehow. It made the whole of the trip, from the stale air of plane after plane to the alien frost of Toronto, feel a little less uncanny.

But the screaming baby knew. The babies always knew.

"I wish Great-Grandfather would learn to use the Internet," she said, shattering the surrounding static of half-understood English with her familiar words. "It's not fair, I know. But you could see him, and speak to him, and say your farewells from a café in Aden. Why you both refuse to learn these things is beyond me. If Great-Grandfather wants to die without a computer or television, it's fine.

I cannot criticize a man who never even warmed to the printed codex. But you are a young woman, Sabiha, and the world is bigger than you know."

At the next gate, another uniformed guard spat some English in a voice demanding obedience.

"Step this way," said Ghada. "You've been selected for another random screening." Her eyes narrowed. She didn't seem to think it was random at all.

"It's their right," said Sabiha, dutifully stepping behind a line of yellow tape. "They are only being careful."

Ghada blinked sharply. "No, you've traveled only two days. You would tire of it very quickly, this hellish carefulness. It gets into your clothes and your hair, in time, the way they treat you. It's why I don't make the trip home anymore, except to fetch you this one time. It's why you'll be going back alone."

"Ghada, you can't be serious!"

"It will be fine. *Ummuna* and Nadheer will get you at the airport."

Sabiha sighed her disapproval. "It's terrible."

"All travel in the West is like this," said Ghada. "I love my sister. Of course I am glad to see you. But you have only begun to learn why you should not have come."

"I'm not afraid," said Sabiha. *Not of that*, she added to herself.

It was two hours before they cleared customs, for reasons neither sister could understand. The dim afternoon had already darkened to night, and luminous fat flakes of snow seemed to race each other to the earth in the orange glow of the lights over the parking lot.

"It's so cold," said Sabiha. "What time is it?"

"It's early, yet," said her sister. "We've got a long way to go."

Sabiha eyed her sister with surprise. "You're driving?"

Ghada gestured to the snow. "Well, we're not walking," she said in English.

The pickup truck was new and shiny, but it turned over sluggishly in the cold. Sabiha cringed as her sister held the key over and forced the engine to something like life.

"Don't break it," said Sabiha. "Nadheer would say, you mustn't break it."

Ghada smiled and let go of the grinding key as the engine smoothed out. "He would also say, you mustn't talk about things you don't know. Canada is my country now, Sabiha. Things are different here. And put on your seat belt."

"Not so different," said Sabiha. "Men are the same most everywhere. Here, women just go about more like men. Do you suppose that makes them easier to understand, or harder?"

"You do not understand my world," snapped Ghada.

"Nor you mine."

They drove in sulking silence for a long time. Resentment turned to silent boredom as the sisters sat alone with their thoughts. Ghada watched the white highway streak by and half-dreamt of a bespectacled man with green eyes that sparkled like gems. He worked in her laboratory, and she wondered if Sabiha might put in a good word with the family, if only she tolerated her sister's absurd journey. She resented them, a little, and wondered if their approval would be so important now. She liked the food here, and had learned all there was to know about winter, and wondered whether she would ever leave.

Far away, on the other side of the truck cab, Sabiha pondered just how little Ghada really knew about winter. She had read many books in the sciences, perhaps, but Sabiha knew that books could no more capture the sound of the wind than a pinned insect the mystic truth of its flight. It would never be quite right, in the end—and thinking about it, once it was written, could drive you mad.

"How far is it to Great-Grandfather's house?" asked Sabiha, when her thoughts had turned to fluttering nightmares, and all the silence she could stand had passed.

"Far as far, and half again," said Ghada. "I have seen it only once, to put him there in the first place. If you understood where we must go, you would never have asked it of me."

"You do not want to take me."

"Of course not," snapped Ghada. "But you are my only sister, and the old fool's only friend. He can hide from all the world, but he cannot hide from the Hour. And no one should die alone."

"Even death may die," breathed Sabiha, caressing the pendant beneath her abaya.

"What was that?" asked Ghada.

"I asked, how far is the drive?" Sabiha lied. "It seems like we have driven for hours."

"We have," said Ghada. "We will be in Cochrane by morning. But the drive is only the beginning."

II.

They passed an endless procession of Western towns, all dominated by squat brick houses and low blocky industrial buildings with dull metal siding. The Christian cathedrals that seemed so vain and grandiose in the city gave way to smaller, humbler facsimiles—queer triangular buildings of snow-covered brick and wood. The low rolling fields turned to immense walls of hard brown rock, through which the long white ribbon of road had slashed like a searing knife. True to Ghada's word, they pulled into Cochrane just after sunrise. In this last morning light, she saw before Ghada replaced her veil that she had aged some, though she was still exquisitely beautiful.

In town, Ghada's English became so rapid-fire with the white men that Sabiha was lost in its bellowing sharpness. They were in a trainyard, loading the truck onto an impossibly long train, paying in thin wads of skinny plastic bills. Above them the wind howled strangely, and Sabiha knew that they had come to a doorway. Great-Grandfather had not lied when he said he was going beyond that most foreign of veils to hear the last verse of the song of the dead. Only now, in these frigid gatelands, did she understand him.

There was more money to come, lots of it. Sabiha had some idea of what it would have bought in Yemen. At a giant yellow discount store by another triangular church, Ghada bought her a winter coat without haggling over price, and maybe without even looking at it. She clucked her tongue dismissively when Sabiha tried to protest.

"I already have a coat," said Sabiha.

"You may think that's a coat," said her sister. "You'll learn soon enough that it isn't."

"I'm only shivering because I'm up all night."

"You'll sleep on the train, and then you'll see that's not so."

In a small restaurant, Ghada with her meticulous English ordered them a breakfast of eggy bread that was something like a plain mutabbaq in a sweet syrup, and they returned to meet a passenger train that looked smaller and far more frightened of the North than its freight-hauling cousin. On plastic seats, jostling over uneven ties, Sabiha lay her head against the rattling window and drifted into sleep as the train trundled away from a country that only hours before had seemed alien to her.

The snow in her dreams may as well have been the white sands of the desert. According to the old hadiths, hellfire could burn both cold and hot; as a child, Sabiha had assumed that if you went round one way far enough, you could reach the other. Great-Grandfather had always flourished in the hellish desert; she recalled now once how she had gone to see him near Damascus as a young girl, she had returned home with her brown hands so badly sunburnt that they shed their skin again and again, like the skin of a desert reptile. He had been a young man of eighty-some years then, and she just a girl. In her dream she was thirteen, sitting on a threadbare carpet in his home, sharing sweets with him from an enormous platter laid out on a woven mat. Great-Grandfather had always had the best sweets; it was, when she was very young, what had made him interesting. But at thirteen, her thoughts had changed.

"Always you eat so many sweets," she said. "How are you so thin when all you eat is honey and cake?"

"I have told you," said Great-Grandfather. "There is a hollowness in me as big as the sky."

"I said the same thing to my mother," she said. "She does not believe it." He only smiled in answer.

She wondered somehow, in the dream, whether these were memories—whether it was a conversation they had had that summer, or whether she only dreamt it now, or whether it had always been there, forgotten, in someplace beyond the noise of the old city. In the dream she took the last cake and chewed it thoughtfully.

"When will you teach me the all the secrets of the wind?"

"All of them?" said Great-Grandfather. "When you turn into a hundred curious children, and when I become a hundred old and dying men."

"Nadheer says you're old and dying now."

"Nadheer speaks the truth," said Great-Grandfather. "Though he does not know it. You are old and dying, too, Sabiha."

"Then when can I know it all?"

"Even I don't know it all," said Nadheer. "It's madness to think of it. I mean it, madness. One day, I will tell you the story of the man who tried to write it all down."

"When, Great-Grandfather? When?"

"When you too hear the wind that howls from beyond the veil, child. When you know a little of why he failed."

"So...after the new year?"

"Yes," he said. "A long time after that."

When the journey's end jostled her awake, the smells of his old house were still fresh in her mind. She wondered how long it had been from that moment to this, and could have counted to her present age, but simple arithmetic would not answer her question. Great-Grandfather had seemed ninety then, she thought, but she wasn't sure. Like an unmarried woman in the market, his true age was an impossible mystery. He might only be ninety now. But if he were only ninety, she thought, he had been ninety for a very long time.

Still with one foot in dream, she clutched her new sleeves tightly and came out of the train with Ghada. A light snow was falling, fat flakes the size of beetles shining peach-pink under the tall station streetlights. Beyond the thin veil of streetlit snow, the day was as black as a crypt.

"What time is it?" Sabiha asked, shivering.

"North," answered her sister.

The cold of snowy Toronto was the distant memory of a summer's day by comparison, so far behind them that she wondered if she had made up the whole thing. Perhaps Toronto had been this cold, after all. Perhaps the desert roads of Yemen were this cold, too. Perhaps it was this cold, all over the world, and always had been, and would be till the very end.

They met the truck at the freightyard across the lot, and sat shivering and burning fuel for a time. Sabiha gripped her pendant tightly. It was nearly hot against her skin, now, and kept the fingers from going numb. She might have fallen asleep again, if Ghada had not wrenched the truck into low gear to follow the truck she had been waiting for—a supply truck with bright tail lights, turning up toward the ice road.

"I understand you, now," said Sabiha. "This *is* a long way."

Ghada smiled. "We haven't driven across the ocean to nowhere, yet. Don't forget your seat belt."

III.

The ice road came only in winter, and only then when the sheet ice over the bay was thick enough to support a supply truck. This was no easy task, for this was no simple lake road, but an uncanny blue-white highway pushing a tireless path across the sea itself. The water here was deep and salty; only a few weeks a year would the road appear. It was a dangerous way, and grew more dangerous every year as some unseen hand of cruelty transformed the world. They drove painfully slow, nothing but flat ice and blackness around them, save the distant tail lights of an experienced rig in the distance—but he soon outpaced them, and then there was nothing. Ghada told her sister, as the drivers had told her, to proceed with a hand on the door at all times, and to be ready to leap onto the ice and crawl away from the truck if she felt the front-end lurch down violently. They might survive on the ice for a half hour or so; the chances of a passerby in that time might be slim, but it was a better end than the deep.

That much Sabiha did not need to be told twice. There was a special end to those who went below, especially in these places beyond the world. She understood, only now, that her sister had not been so unwise, so utterly unschooled in the howling of the wind. She could hear it in the infinite black above them, now that it was too cold even for snow, screaming against the cab of the truck.

"Your courage is great in coming here," said Sabiha.

"I'm past courage and into madness," said Ghada, knuckles tight on the wheel, one hand on the door. "It runs in the family. I'm crazy as Great-Grandfather. Crazier, even. I can't imagine why he came up here to die. But there's a certain sense, when you go somewhere to die, choosing a place that will kill you. I don't yearn for such things, Sabiha. I yearn for my book to be published, and for handsome Jason in my laboratory to notice me, and for Nadheer to approve of my marrying a Westerner someday. All things that will not happen if we go down through the ice. Everything Great-Grandfather wants in death, he is going to get. Everything Ghada wants in life, Ghada's going to lose."

There was a warmth in Ghada's complaining, as if they were young together again, as if two sisters lamenting the unkindness of life to each other were the most natural and human thing in the world. They passed the timeless journey as the kindred sisters they had once been, and their laughter warmed the cab at last. It was dark beyond dark, now, and the headlights and instruments and the two women's smiles gave off the only light in all existence, like a single dwarf star trembling in the merciless void of night.

On the far side of eternity lay a town. A few flickering lights there carried a long way into the cloudless, snowless night. Beneath their welcoming glow, the ice road turned again to gravel and wound through rows of metal homes like tiny airplane hangars. The Northern store where they parked the truck looked like the same design, built of the same materials—only scaled up like a mothership.

"Remember we are only guests on this land," said Ghada. She raised her veil and tied her scarf over it. It took several hard pushes to unstick the frozen doors.

It was clear Ghada expected her to be uncomfortable here, but after the long night on the ice road, the supermarket was like coming home. The fluorescent lights offered the illusion, at least, of warmth, and the women who shopped among the onions and crates of oranges were likewise attired— leggings under long dresses, immense puffy coats, heads wrapped under hats, faces scarved, eyes beautiful and glistening like dark gems. It was the first place in the West she felt as if she could have talked to anybody, even in English.

Ghada bought them some fruit that had once been fresh. Sabiha could tell from her sister's body language that it was very expensive. But it gave her an excuse to talk to the cashier, a pretty raven-haired girl who looked surprised to see them, but not wary.

"I'm looking for Michael Billy," said Ghada, handing over her purchases. "Do you know him?"

The girl nodded. "You're here to see the Arab," she said, smiling brightly with recognition. "Both of you?" It was a kinder reaction, here at the top of the world, where maybe no Arabs had ever been but Great-Grandfather, than Sabiha had seen anywhere in the city that supposedly housed fifty thousand of them.

"Yes," said Ghada.

"I'll find Mike for you," she said. The clerk at the next register rang them through as the girl bounced away, and Ghada exchanged pleasantries while Sabiha studied the store, transfixed by the bright colours after what felt like a century of night.

The girl's cheeks were rosy from the cold when she returned, bringing a round-faced man with shaggy hair and a catfish smile, dressed up like a pillbug in a puffy blue coat with, of all things, a baseball cap.

"Hey stranger," he said in English. "It's been a long time."

"Hello," said Ghada. Sabiha could tell she was disarmed by the man's friendliness; she was, too, a little.

"And this is your first time," he said. "I'm Mike. I've been looking after the old man." Sabiha extended a gloved hand timidly, as she had been taught, and he shook it hard and enthusiastically. It felt odd, made her feel manly.

"How is he?" asked Ghada.

Mike shook his shaggy head, though his cheer diminished only a little. "Not so good," he said. "He's been real down since you called up. He'll be glad to see you. I think you'll be glad you came in time. Are you tired? I can take you up now, if you want. I can carry you both, if you don't mind crowding."

Ghada nodded. "We should go." They ate their bananas there in the store while Mike talked about the weather and asked Sabiha about Yemen.

"Are you staying long?" he asked them. When Ghada shook her head, he nodded sagely.

"It's maybe for the best," he said. "People here, not everybody's so welcoming to white folks."

Sabiha let out a shy laugh. She'd never quite imagined herself as white.

The snowmobile was sleek and alien, like a black-shelled bug, and it roared so loud that Mike had to shout to be heard over the engine, which seemed to suit him just fine.

"Your granddad doesn't come down much," he called over the engine and the crunchy scrabbling of the treads. "Never, now. I take his groceries maybe once every couple of weeks, that seems to do him. He doesn't bother nobody, and nobody's unkind to him. They think he's a little nuts, of course. In town they just call him the Mad Arab. I hope that's not offensive."

Neither woman spoke up over the engine, so after a minute of silence, he saw fit to continue.

"Can't say I blame them," Mike shouted. "The Old Town got washed away in a flood, years on years ago. I was just a kid. I barely remember it. But lots of us didn't make it. I was in my bed, and it was like a big wet hand with a thousand fingers come up out of the deep, fell over us. *Wham!* Took everything. The houses, the boats. All but one little house, a shack, my old uncle's shack. Wasn't even the highest building. It's down by the sea. There were houses up on the rock, it took 'em right off. My uncle's house, it flooded clear up to the roof, but it didn't wash up. Didn't break away. Good foundations, they said. So anyway, that's where your granddad lives now. Maybe just waiting to get washed away his own self. Why would a man do that? It don't make sense. It's mad. So we call him the Mad Arab. We don't mean anything by it."

Sabiha nodded as they slowed over poorer terrain, and felt bold enough, now, to shout herself.

"Why do you do it?" she asked. "Why do you let him squat up there?"

"He pays for his food," shouted Mike. "He's got money. But I guess—it's important to him, is all. Whatever reason he came up here, whatever he got away from, it's gotta be the most important thing in the world. I can respect that."

"We don't know, either," said Ghada—though Sabiha knew, of course. "He's crazy to us, too."

"My uncle died," said Mike, "saving the kids from that flood. The government—Indian Affairs, it was called back then—you know what his kids got? Bugger. They got bugger. 'Cause his house, that piece of shit house your granddad's in, that house is still standing." He swallowed hard. "So whatever fool thing's important to him, I respect it, even if I don't understand. I guess I wish, maybe one time, somebody'd respected what was important to me."

"That's why you bring him chicken and oranges."

"He does pay," said Mike. "But yeah. That's why."

At the end of the world, there was a rocky promontory, not very high above the sea, and on that promontory there was a small wooden house. Mike stopped well back from the house, as he always did unless there was something heavy to carry.

"I'll let you go here," he said. "Give the old man my best. I'll come back for you when that storm's run its course." He gestured toward the black sky, toward the billion trillion stars hanging suspended over the house, toward some phantom storm that the women could not see. Sabiha knew, then, that this smiling grocery-man was one who knew, too, though perhaps not in the same way. He was the only the second man she had met, after Great-Grandfather, who did.

"Come on," said Ghada. "I've been awake so long, I just want to lie on a bed. And if Great-Grandfather is in it, I'll roll him on the floor."

IV.

Great-Grandfather's face was as hollow as an old drum, and the skin stretched hard across its surface was just as dry. He'd been handsome enough once, for a spry man of ninety, with cheeks full of joy in spite of the spectral black depths of his eyes. But a monstrous war against time had been fought on that face; great trenches were dug in the slope of his forehead, and his cheeks and the flesh beneath his sunken eyes had been driven off the field. His teeth, too, those monuments of an ancient time, had been smashed and thrown down like the toppled white idols of the gods of the vanquished. Only his tremendous and sagely nose stood victorious against time; where it had once merely dominated his lean features with its aggressive presence, there was now no scrap of terrain left in that face of ages that it did not seem to command.

He opened the door with his left hand and greeted them with his right. Sabiha was tall enough now to kiss his forehead, and lowered her veil to do so out of respect. The cold of the perpetual night stung her cheeks immediately; he seemed to sense her discomfort and waved her inside.

The house was little more than a cabin, heated and somewhat lit by a wood stove. Someone, perhaps him, had put in a handful of electric lights, but the generator beside the old shack was silent as death. There was a crate of oranges on the table— no doubt a luxury here—surrounded by a heap of dried peels. Sabiha knew without asking they were all he had been eating.

They exchanged their pleasantries; and true to her word, Ghada stripped off her outer layers even as she spoke to him. His bed was a simple box-spring and mattress by the stove, and she was curled beneath the blankets before they had finished talking.

"We've come so far," she said. "I'm not used to all this. We'll talk in the morning."

"Morning will come in nineteen days," said her grandfather, but she was already too far away in dream to acknowledge him.

"She has been tremendous," said Sabiha softly. "I had no idea. I did not know you had come so far."

Great-Grandfather took down an old wooden matchbox from a high shelf. "This is the edge of the world," he said. "I had to come here."

"You said once there were many edges of the world."

"Just so," he said. "There are edges even in the Old City. You can walk to the edge of the world from your brother's door. But I had to come here, because you had to come here."

"I don't understand," said Sabiha.

"But you think you do," said Great-Grandfather. He pulled a small bundle of dried plants from the matchbox and, gingerly opening the door to the wood stove, tossed it into the fire. Almost at once a pungent and warming scent began to fill the cabin.

"What is that?"

"It will help her dream," he said. "Come down with me to where the sea is darkest."

They left the house; Sabiha had not replaced her veil, for she was with family; but the cold did not seem to bother her for long. Indeed, as they left the house behind them and came down the slope of a barren hill, the biting air came to bother her less and less.

"It's not cold," she said, a little surprised.

"It's very cold," her Grandfather said. "But you have come through the coldness of the Earth, and this is not that. Against this, you are protected. I made sure of it."

Sabiha gently brushed the pendant beneath her abaya. "Are you cold?"

"To the bone," he said. "But you are here, and my comfort no longer matters." He gestured to a small pile of firewood stacked against the side of the cabin as they came down the hill and it passed from view. "That is my firewood, the last of it. I awoke one morning two weeks ago to find my bones are too weak, now, to swing the hatchet. You came just in time for your last lesson."

"You mean my first lesson," Sabiha said. "I have waited all my life for my first lesson."

Great-Grandfather's bright, half-toothed smile of fallen idols gleamed an eerie shade of green. At first she thought she had imagined it, and then that it was some trick of his sorcery. But he did not work in such vulgar terms; he was many things, but a magician was not one of them.

"See with your larger eyes," he said.

They had come down to a barren and rocky place, a shallow promontory of mottled stone whose edges were lapped at by the patient black waters of an eerily calm ocean. The stars that had once shone so brightly overhead had faded, now, veiled behind a curtain of shimmering light that streaked across the empty sky. Cascading ribbons of radiant green filled the sky with their power, as thunderous in their majesty as they were silent in their wordless sermon.

Sabiha's mouth drifted gently open. She breathed in sharply, as if gasping for light.

"You have begun without me," Great-Grandfather said, though his tone was gentle. "You went to Damascus, as the Servant of the Forbidden did. Where Ghada sought the sciences of this world, you looked always to the night, hoping to peer behind that most foreign of veils, to look upon the faces of those who dwell beyond the stars."

"I have waited my whole life," she breathed.

"You have not waited at all," he answered. "I warned you, as a girl, that to consign these living things to dead books is to kill them with lies, and they do not like being killed any more than you or I. And so you have wisely stayed out of the footsteps of my own great-grandfather—the footsteps that drove him first mad, and then to something worse."

"I have remembered your words always," she said. "There is no truth in any book but what we bring into it."

"And if you do not learn from books—then where does truth come from?"

"From the world," she said. "And from beyond."

"You speak of the Outsiders."

"Yes."

"We have come to their door now," said Great-Grandfather, and she saw that it was true. "You have passed through the cruelty of men, through the cruelty of the Earth itself, to the place where you had thought you might speak to infinity. And I know what you expected to find there."

She had expected to find the truth—the sort of truth that screaming babies know, the sort that short-lived men of temporal power did not. She had imagined the terrible future, the ineffable eldritch names howled faintly upon a wind that blew from stranger skies than the dumb and simple blackness of space—the wind of the very breath of the slumbering Elders in their palaces beyond the night.

That, she was sure, was the howling wind of her ancestor—the wind of forbidden truths. She was certain of it. That was always how it went, in every story she had ever heard. She might go mad, but she would learn the truth of the beyond.

"And what do you hear?"

Silence.

She stood on the doorstep of the infinite void—and nothing was there.

It seemed foolish, in that moment, utterly stupid, to imagine something in the void.

"Nothing exists in the void," she said. "That's why they call it the *void*."

Great-Grandfather nodded, and spoke the simple words it had taken his lifetime to discover:

"The Outsiders," he said, "are not at home."

The cultish madness Sabiha had encountered came in many ways. Like any garden-variety death cult of the Americas, there were many who conflated death, destiny, and the divine, many who firmly believed their gods would eat them, or call the souls up from their bodies, or end them in some other grisly way. It was the way of cultish thinking to embrace this abhorrence, to long for it. There was a cultivated comfort in seeing that terrible destiny through: with her own eyes, while trying to get back to Sana'a, she had seen men immolated alive in their homes, men dead of shells or shrapnel or worse things who went out of the world with faces contorted in weird serenity. To believe in the Eldest, she knew, was to believe in a fate of unimaginable horror—but even so, there was a comfort in going to meet it. The shape of her end had long been unknowable to her—and there was a warmth, at least, in *knowing*.

But there was nothing to know in that silence.

It was somehow worse.

Great-Grandfather had lowered himself down on the rock with a sense of finality. He did not expect to stand up again.

"The rest you will discover in time," he said. "You are a smart girl. Silly things like alchemy, geomancy, numbers and ciphers and forgotten names—those are simple tricks. You can learn to palm a card, too, or escape handcuffs, if it suits you. But you are about to learn the last of what I know—and it will be your burden alone to answer the question that comes of it."

If truth does not come from books—where does truth live?

When she was thirteen, he would test her with riddles—games about lions and goats, puzzles whose answers were the moon, or the wind in the reeds.

Truth must live outside of books.

"I don't want you to die," she said, a note of human affection breaking her voice slightly. "You are still my Great-Grandfather, and I am still a girl who loves you very much."

"I'm awfully old," said Great-Grandfather.

"You've been ninety as long as I can remember," said Sabiha. "You can be ninety a while longer, I think."

If the Eldest do not lie slumbering outside the world—where do they dwell?

"I quite like being ninety," he said. "People treat you with kindness. Men of far tribes, and women of other families, are no longer frightened of you. You eat less and sleep more. It's quite nice. But no, Sabiha. You are finishing now your last lesson. You are learning your first secret. And I must be ready to die, for such things never come without payment."

Sabiha felt the cold of the Earth again, a cold against which her pendant brought little warmth. It came all at once—the coldness of the spraying ocean, the frost in the eyes of the men in the airport, the terrible chill of the wind that had come up around them suddenly, as if from nowhere— the storm that Mike had predicted, that she had forgotten entirely in the stillness of her lesson. Her face was stung by water that turned to knives of ice in the air; she tasted blood on her lips, and in that moment the shimmering beauty of the green skies seemed a sharp contrast to a world steeped in an unassailable cruelty and malevolent will.

They were here, of course.

Now.

Perhaps they always had been. Perhaps the cruelty of mankind had been the howl of the insect wind all along.

The world roared as the black sea threw up a many-fingered hand, torn suddenly from its mooring among the rocks as the screaming wind struck a change in the tide. Under the thunderous incandescence of the aurora, Sabiha saw that they had not come down so far from the cabin after all; it really was just on a low rock overlooking the ocean some distance north. She saw the darkness of the icy depths come up like a thousand-headed serpent, a lashing, writhing, living scourge that flayed the rock in a steady stream and, with the aggressive deftness of a Bara'a war dancer, plucked the little cabin off the rock as effortlessly as a child picking a berry, heaving it headlong into the sea. Sabiha had the breath to call her sister's name only once before she was whelmed, too, by a claw of ocean water that knocked her from her feet with its force and blasted the air from her lungs with its chill alone. Great-Grandfather, who had been lying prone, was spared the worst of it, but he looked up with surprise, and sadness, and no small guilt as the little house was smashed to pieces on the crags by waves fighting like wolves over scraps.

"I suppose one can live a long time," he said as Sabiha slipped away into unconsciousness, "and still not know everything."

V.

Michael Billy knew his coastal windstorms. He could smell them coming up almost out of nowhere, and could predict them even in the dead of winter when the sky couldn't hold a cloud. But even he didn't know how bad it would be until it was tearing the shingles off his roof and knocking out the village generators with surprising ferocity. He didn't waste time in getting on the phone before the lines went down, and once the Coast Guard was on its way, he rallied his brother Shane and went out himself. In a hospital in the inlet perhaps a hundred miles down the coast, Sabiha learned that his quick action probably snatched her back from the jaws of death—and it troubled her more, now, to think what death might mean now that the whole world was a dwelling place for things that ought never to have stirred from beyond the veil of night. The howling of the wind was with her still; it had drowned out even the rotors of the air ambulance, and robbed her of sleep.

In very slow English, it was explained that the blisters on her hands and feet were from the frostbite, but they had managed to save her fingers and toes. She had ruptured an eardrum in the storm or the fall, and needed a few stitches to close the gash on her head, but after they warmed her up and stabilized her that was the worst of it.

Search and Rescue had dredged up what was left of Ghada's mangled body within the first nine hours. There was no word or sign of Great-Grandfather.

The nurses watched her recovery with hostile dark eyes. It was clear they believed she should never have been there—none of them should have. One of them even went so far as to say it: "you should've stayed in the desert." But the roar in Sabiha's ear was nearly too loud to hear it, and she was too numb with grief to care in any case.

When the time finally came, she expected the trip home to be a lonely one. Her English had improved, but it was still weak. She had booked, at great expense, an empty seat for Ghada, and she would have to break the news to Nadheer and